I will call it ...

FAR
FAR
AWAY
BOOKS

2012

SAD TALES FOR ME

A Bio**DO**graphy *

by James Barklee (me)

If lost, please return to:
12 Basketville Chase,
Much Drooling, Barkshire

---

* **biodography** (bai-dog-ra-fee) *n.* An account of a canine's life, written by another. First used by James Barklee in 2012.
It should be an autobiodography but that's just too wordy for a small dog like me.

When you're small it's easy to be
overlooked.

But even an underdog like me has
something to say ...

In the beginning, I was curled up
with my nose nuzzled in my mum's warm
fur, breathing her safe scent.

Then she was gone and I found myself
alone ...

... waiting.

My family likes to think they chose
me but really, I chose them.

I simply **wagged** myself into their life.

How could they resist?

I soon made myself at home.
Comfy bed, cosy blanket ...

... shiny new bowl.

I **love** my bowl.

Except ...

... the service can be a bit slow.

What's a dog got to do
to get some food around here?

At first, my family thought I was
growling when I flashed them my best
smile.

Now my grins are met with

laughter

and, "You're such an ugly dog, James!"

Inside I'm beautiful.

Sometimes, I wish they could see it, too.

I know they feel safe with me around.

Almost as soon as I arrived, a smart
new sign appeared on the door ...

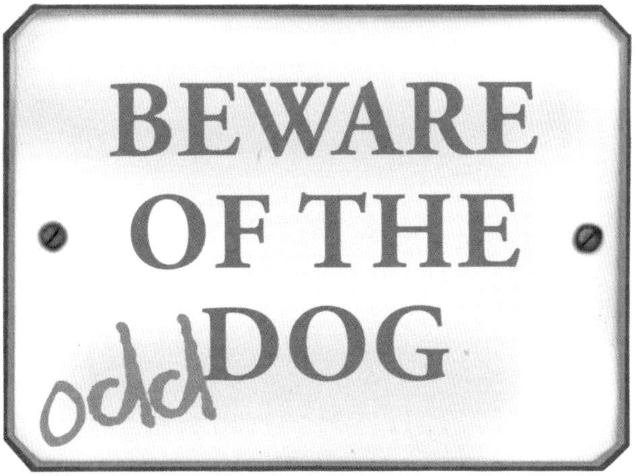
BEWARE
OF THE
odd DOG

But when you're small, it's hard to be taken seriously as a guard dog. Living up to high expectations is tricky, unless you have a little help, of course.

Good bye mild-mannered James, hello wicked me. Watch out ...

... SNAP! SNAP!
... SNAP! SNAP!

My family tells me I'm a watchdog.

So I sit and watch.

Sometimes my job takes moments.

Other times, a whole day ...

... depending on who ...

or what ...

I'm watching ...

At night, it's eerily quiet.

The house is almost completely still.

So I sit and play with my shadow.
Which is fun ...

... until it decides to play, too.

Then my shadow grOWS scary!

So I dash undercover, hiding beneath
my blanket, paws over my ears and eyes
squeezed tightly shut, till morning
comes ...

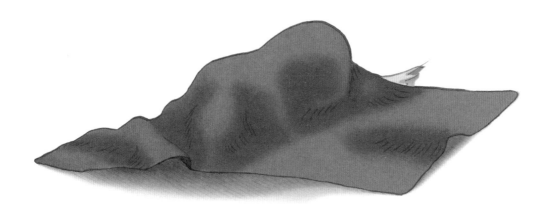

... and it's safe to come out again.

On bright, sunny mornings
I love hunting.

Bug-hunting.

Sometimes, it's hard to tell if

I'm chasing them ....

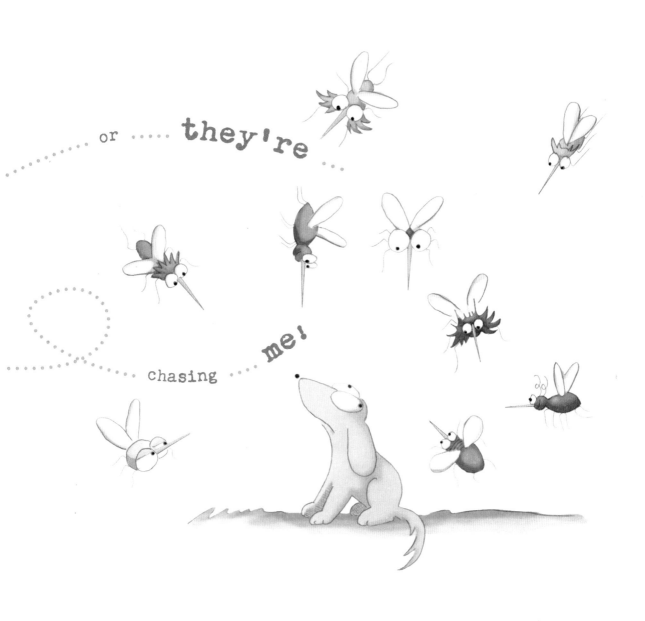

But there are worse things
than bugs.

A clash with Titan, for example.

He's a dog whose bite is a **lot** worse
than his bark.

My family says I should
toughen up -

mark my territory.

So I do and they shout,
"No! Bad dog!"

Sometimes, I don't understand
people at all.

I get called 'bad dog' a lot.

When I play with the kitten ...

... when I help myself to a snack ...

... if I play in mud ...

... when I bark to protect my family ...

... **and** when I don't.

My opinion doesn't seem to count.
They say it's washday.

I say my blanket **smells** fine the way it is.

jump jump jump jump jump jump jump jump jump jump jump j

I may be small, but I can jump like a flea.
It's handy when I want to get noticed.

jump jump jump jump jump

jump jump jump jump jump jump jump jump jump jump jump jump

boing

When it's vet-time, I'd rather they **didn't** see me.

I make myself as
small
as possible
and hide.

The vet says I have 'small dog syndrome'.
That's easy for her to say,
towering over me in her...

heels

Small people have it easy.

Even my love life isn't straightforward.
I fell in love the moment I saw
those big, blue eyes.

She may be a cat ...

... but you can't help who you
fall in love with.

Nor can you choose your relations.
When I'm with my doggy family, people
stop and point.

"All the dogs round here are so alike!"
they laugh.

At first glance, maybe.
But I'm different.
I'm going places ...

... whenever I can.

As soon as the front gate is open
I seize my chance.

I run for miles, through the streets
to the park.

Exciting smells rush at me, as I
scamper here and there ...

... sniffing greedily.

pitter .... patt...

I chase the squirrels, scattering them across the grass and into the woods ...

dash

skitter ... scatter ...

skitter ... hurry .... scurry ...

swerve ... rush ...

... just because I can.

Round and round I run in the cool,
dark shade, chasing anything
that moves.

Birds, rabbits and the leaves on the breeze.

Following my nose always gets me into
trouble.

What a foolish dog I've been.
One whiff of freedom ...

... and I'm lost!

My heart hammers.

I desperately search for a familiar scent.

The smell of my family.

pine cones · · · · · · · · · · · · ·

bark · · · · · · · · · ·

many rabbits · · · · · · · · · · · · · ·

· · · · · · · · · · ·

hairy bugs · · · · · · · ·

two rabbits

· · · · · two rabbits

damp leaves · · · · · · worms

They always find me in the end.
I flash them my best smile as they
sweep me into a big **cuddle** and hot
tears splash my fur.

I realise I am **loved.** And I know
that despite their faults, and mine

... we are **meant** to be together.

At home, I don't fuss too much when they make me have a bath.

Well, just a little, in case they think I like it.

They might make me have one every week.

When you're small - especially a
small dog like me - it's easy to feel
overlooked and misunderstood.

But, as we settle down in front of
the fire, I smile. My mishaps and sad
tales end happily ...

... because my family **loves** me;
eccentric, individual me, just as I
love them, faults and all.

It's a dog's life, and **I** wouldn't
change it for the **world** ...

Editor's note:

This manuscript was found in a park
and was of much interest to publishers
and dog-experts alike. Extensive searches
were made, during which time many dogs came
forward to claim it as their work.

The real James Barklee was tracked down
to his home where he lives happily with his
family, who were completely unaware that
their dog could read and write.

Reuben: thank you for allowing me to be me.
Without your care and support I couldn't have
done this. You stood by me, grumbling, but
there. Even when I was more annoying than
a bad case of fleas.

Alexandre: my inspiration. Thank you from
the bottom of my doggy heart, for the idea
and the wonderful title. Thank you for your
encouragement, smiles and care, but most
of all for feeding me on time!

Saphir: with blue eyes my heart swims in;
my soulmate, best friend and playmate.

www.farfarawaybooks.com

With thanks to Sue McMillan for brushing up my canine text
and to Alison Gadsby, Gill McLean, Nuno Fonseca and Carlos Vieira Reis
for working their design magic on my doggy drawings and pages

First published in Great Britain in 2012 by Far Far Away Books and Media, Ltd.
20-22 Bedford Row, London, WC1 R4S

Copyright © Far Far Away Books and Production

Text and illustrations copyright © 2011 by James Barklee
The moral right of James Barklee to be identified as the author
and the illustrator of this work has been asserted.

Edited by Sue McMillan
Cover by Alison Gadsby
Graphic design by Alison Gadsby, Nuno Fonseca, Gill McLean, Carlos Vieira Reis
ISBN: 978-1-908786-00-5
A CIP catalogue record for this book is available from the British Library

Printed and bound in Portugal
by Printer Portuguesa

FSC
www.fsc.org
MIX
Paper from
responsible sources
FSC® C006423

info@farfarawaybooksandmedia.co.uk

FAR FAR
FAR FAR
AWAY
BOOKS

2012